'012

HEATHER PATTERSON MARY JANE GERBER

Thanks for Thanksgiving

Scholastic Canada Ltd.

Toronto New York London Auckland Sydney
Mexico City New Delhi Hong Kong Buenos Aires

To my parents —
who first showed me
the beauty of nature
and the nature of love.
— *H.P.*

To Ted, Patrick, Rebekah
and our buddy Zip.
I give thanks for you all.
— *M.J.G.*

Scholastic Canada Ltd.
604 King Street West, Toronto, Ontario, M5V 1E1 Canada

Scholastic Inc.
557 Broadway, New York, NY 10012, USA

Scholastic Australia Pty Limited
PO Box 579, Gosford, NSW 2250, Australia

Scholastic New Zealand Limited
Private Bag 94407, Greenmount, Auckland, New Zealand

Scholastic Children's Books
Euston House, 24 Eversholt Street,
London NW1 1DB, UK

Canadian Cataloguing in Publication Data

Patterson, Heather, 1945-
Thanks for Thanksgiving

ISBN 0-590-12484-6

1. Thanksgiving day — Juvenile poetry. 2. Children's poetry, Canadian (English)*
I. Gerber, Mary Jane. II. Title.

PS8581.A788T42 1998   jC811'.54   C98-931028-0

PR9199.3.P37T42 1998

ISBN-10 0-590-12484-6 / ISBN-13 978-0-590-12484-3

8 7 6   Printed in Singapore   08 09 10

Thanks for
the warm fall sun.

Thanks for
the outdoor fun.

Thanks for the blue fall sky

and the sound of
the birds' good-bye.

Thanks for
the golden trees.

Thanks for the crunch of leaves.

Thanks for
the Northern Spys

that turn into apple pies.

Thanks for the special meal

16

and the loving way we feel.

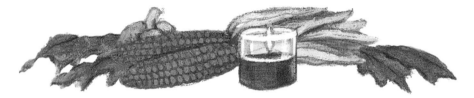

Thanks for the wonderful smell.

It's time for the dinner bell!

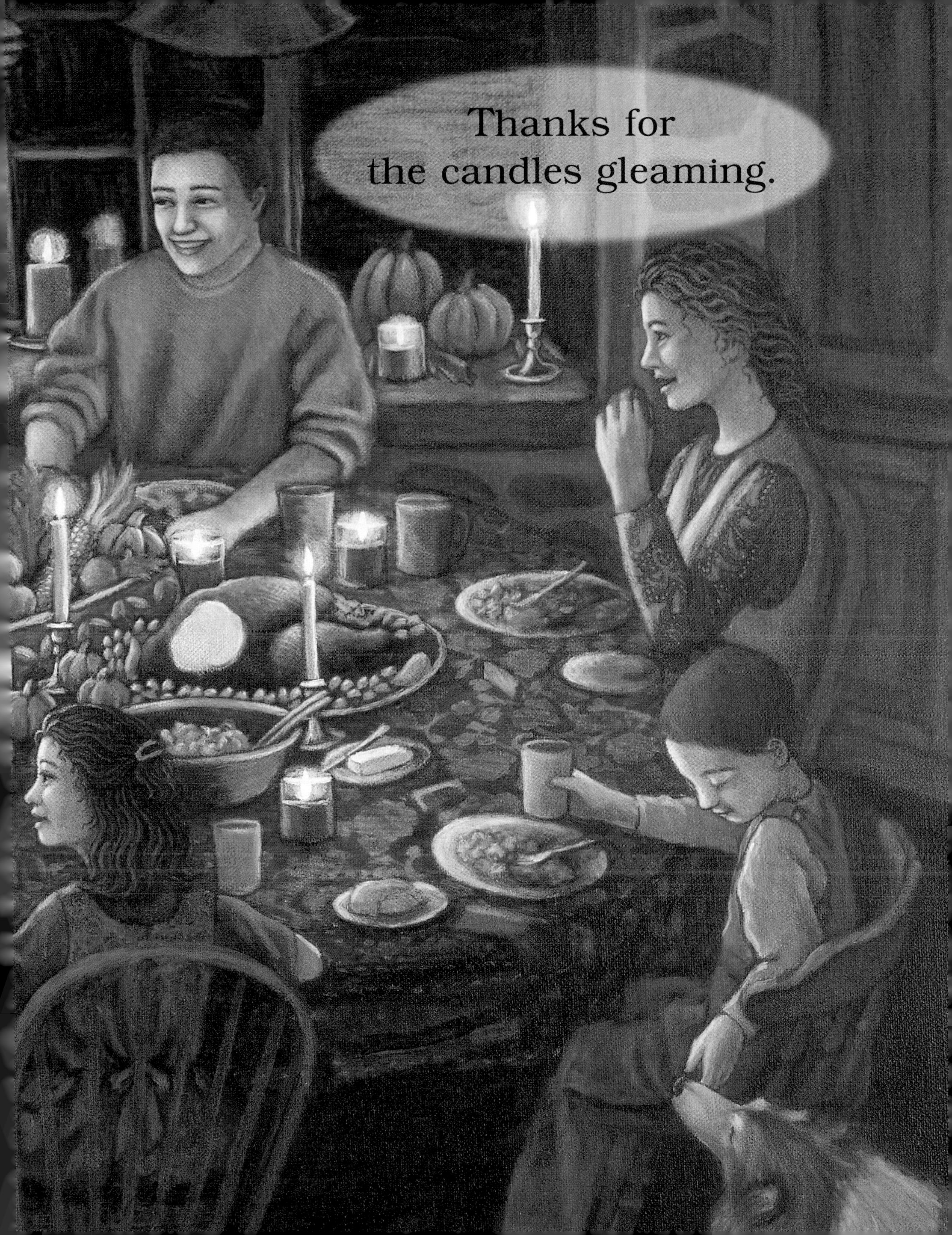

Thanks for
the candles gleaming.

Thanks for the faces beaming.

Thanks for the pumpkins bright.
Thanks for the cool fall night.

Thanks for Thanksgiving!

About Thanksgiving in Canada

Every year since 1957, Canadians have celebrated a national holiday on the second Monday of October. We call it Thanksgiving. In 1879, when Parliament first declared Thanksgiving a national holiday, it was on November 6th, and the date changed several times after that. But it has always been a day we share with family and friends, a day we pause to pay tribute to what Parliament called "the bountiful harvest with which Canada has been blessed."

The origins of the holiday are mixed. Long ago, farmers in Europe would fill a curved goat's horn with fruit and grain to give thanks for the abundance of food at harvest time. In 1578, Martin Frobisher held the first "Canadian" feast of thanksgiving for surviving the long journey from England to Labrador. Samuel de Champlain formed the Order of Good Cheer in 1606, and shared the French settlers' feast of thanks with his Micmac neighbours. The Pilgrims celebrated their first harvest in the New World in 1621 at Plymouth, Massachusetts, influenced by the harvest ceremonies of the local Wampanoag tribe. By the 1750s this celebration had reached Nova Scotia, and soon British Empire Loyalists brought it to other parts of the country.

The traditional Thanksgiving dinner we sit down to enjoy together has its origins in the unique foods of this new found land — the wild turkey, cornbread, cranberries, squash and pumpkin that formed the basis of this special feast hundreds of years ago.

And through all the years, the sentiment at the heart of Thanksgiving remains the same — a joyous celebration of food and family, fortune and friends.